Brielle's Promise

Horse Gone Silent Trilogy

Book 3

Shane Ledyard

Published by Shane Ledyard

First Paperback Edition: February 2020

Ledyard, Shane, 1976-

Brielle's Promise: a novella / by Shane Ledyard-1st edition

Edited by Catherine Stone

Summary: *Brielle's Promise* brings together the *Horse Gone Silent* trilogy in the sweetest of ways that no one could have ever imagined. Emma Sterling is back, and she brings with her a surprise that shocks everyone that knows her-even Ophelia! This exciting conclusion to the highly acclaimed *Horse Gone Silent* trilogy will satisfy you and warm your heart, as you return to the stable at Hound Hollow and Emma's hometown, then make an unpredictable stop with new characters that will have you raving for *Brielle's Promise!*

ISBN 9798610815602 (Paperback)

Printed in the United States of America

This book is dedicated to Kevin "Poppy" Rosencrance, who always taught us to keep smiling and to keep moving forward.

CONTENTS

"For God has not given us a spirit of fear, but of power and of love and of a sound mind."

~ 2 Timothy 1:7

Chapter 1

Sleeping Dog
As told by Emma Sterling

A dull, gray November sky loomed over me during the short walk to my house. The incessant chatter on the bus ride home from school had scattered my thoughts, leaving me consumed with worry about my parent's reaction to my pending announcement. I sensed with dread that misunderstanding and guilt were imminent. I couldn't bear the thought of hurting them, but I knew in my heart that I had to tell them what I believed was the right thing for me to do. Even though it might hurt them very, very much.

A frigid breeze nipped at me, so I sped up, breaking into a jog as I passed the grove of towering white pines that stood at the corner of our property. For a reason I could never decipher, nearly every time I passed that particular spot, a menacing feeling would work its way from my stomach to my throat, giving me chills and the feeling that I needed to pass there as quickly as I could. The old farmhouse across the street, with its shade-less windows – which seemed like a portal to someplace grave and dark – gave me an uneasy feeling too. I sprinted to the porch and took the stairs two at a time, leaving notions of leering ghosts behind me. I immediately, albeit temporarily, shook my wretched apprehension, when I burst through the door of our kitchen to be overwhelmed with the warm, comforting smell of fresh baked apple bread.

"Emma girl!" my dad exclaimed. He always made it a point to greet me in the sweetest of ways that made me feel loved.

"Hi Daddy."

"How was the day for the most wonderful eight-grader in the world?"

"Okay, Daddy," I replied, my guilt mounting as his kindness poured over me. "Where's Momma?"

"Oh, she works the eleven to seven shift at the hospital tonight so she's getting a quick nap in before dinner. I'll get to supper as soon as I am done with my last batch of apple bread."

"You are really getting into this whole baking thing," I grinned.

"I'm glad I have a good hobby again. Working at the nursery with all the plants is fun, but it is still a job. When I was a teenager, my first job was in a bakery; I always loved the process of making things for others and the hope of making people happy with something simple."

I looked around the kitchen and saw there had to be two dozen loaves cooling on the counter.

"Daddy, who is all this for?"

"I'm making bread for everyone at my work for Christmas. We'll freeze them in foil until we're ready to give them out."

He beamed as he handed me a big piece. "But don't worry honey, you can have some now."

"Thank you, Daddy," I replied. The first bite tasted like how I imagine fall would taste; implicitly warm, with little bits of apples, cinnamon, and sugar.

"It is so good!" I exclaimed, forgetting my concerns for a moment.

"Are you going to start your homework, Emma girl?"

"Actually," I hesitated, and he caught my look of uncertainty.

"What's on your mind? Is everything all right at school?"

3

"Yes, school is fine. Actually, I was thinking I would take Duke for a walk out back in the woods."

"Sure," he replied with some hesitation, "just remember it gets dark soon, Emma girl. You have maybe an hour."

"Okay, Daddy. Wait, where *is* Duke?"

"He's upstairs with your Momma," he explained and let out a quick, sharp whistle, bringing Duke scampering wildly downstairs. He slid sideways at the base of the steps and hit an end table, sending a plume of hair and dust into the air that drifted poetically through the afternoon sunshine that glowed through the windows of our Victorian home. He scurried to regain his balance, his nails scratching in all directions on the hardwood floors, creating an audible chaos that made us giggle. Duke finally made his way to me, his little border collie body wiggling wildly as he wagged his tail exuberantly.

"Want to go for a walk, boy?"

He stood up on his hind legs and did a half pirouette to show his approval. I opened the door and he ran out in front of me, pausing in the driveway to see which way I wanted to go.

"See you soon Daddy," I said brightly as I closed the door, leaving the comforting smell of the apple bread behind me to face the darkening November sky. I hesitated momentarily, second guessing my decision. I pushed on though, remembering how much I wanted to get to my secret spot in the woods where I knew I could think, and somehow get the courage to tell them what I believed to be right.

Duke ran alongside me as we made our way across the yard and under the willow tree that still held some leaves from the summer, although they were now scant and brown. I reached up and took ahold of a few of the twisting, weeping branches as I walked by. I let them slide through my hands like a rope as I walked, pulling the dead leaves off and letting them drift from my hand and then to the ground, where they would eventually blow away from where they had lived happily all summer.

We reached the cornfield, which was cut down for the summer, now just showing the stumps of the cornstalks. I thought about how Daddy said it's great cover for pheasants, and I hoped perhaps Duke and I would flush one out. The clinking of the metal tags on his collar may have given too much warning though, as we only saw two deer in the distance, running away, their white tails waving as if to say goodbye as they leaped through the brush, the pricker bushes crunching as they made their way out of sight.

We crossed the corn field quickly, the woods inviting us in as the sun rays diminished and the limbs of the trees started to move in a malevolent manner, looking more like veins coursing through the body of a monster rather than part of something green and beautiful that gave us shade from the searing summer sun. Nevertheless, I felt drawn in and made my way down a steep hill, halfway to the creek and sat down on a fallen tree that I had found over the summer when my new friend from the barn and I went exploring. On one of our adventures we had found an old, waterproof metal box. It was quite a plain box, with some rust on the edges and dirt that was caked on the sides from years of being left in the forest. Despite the wear, the box was still very useful. We hid it under the tree in a hollow that was formed by the root structure after the antique oak had fallen. We kept our diaries in it, along with anything else we wanted to keep secret. Our hiding spot was perfect. The creek made just enough noise to cover our voices and we were far enough down the hill that no one could see us from the fields. We were close enough to home to feel safe, but far enough away to feel as though we could be lost forever.

Duke sat beside me as I opened the box and ran my finger across the bracelet that I had left inside. It was a leather bracelet with a brass plate, like a show horse's halter. The inscription read "Best Friends, The Three Of Us." I ran my hand across the face of it a few times and sighed. Duke looked up at me with a compassionate but puzzled look.

"I don't know boy. What do you think?"

He tilted his head and looked even more confused. I reached down and stroked his long, soft fur while I stared at the moon peeking through the trees. I knew that was a sign to get back home as to not worry my parents. I took a deep breath and watched it dissipate into the night sky, opened the box once more, and put the bracelet back inside. As soon as the old box closed, I was overwhelmed with a mixture of conviction and sadness that I had never felt before. I thought about my summer; each and every detail, and everything wonderful that had happened. I thought of my new friends, of the horses, and our adventures together. Images of Ophelia flooded my mind from the last few years-everything we had accomplished despite our rough start and the accident that nearly took her from me. I could see her eyes drowning me in her sweetness and her concern for me when I was having a rough day. Then I thought of my friend, buried my face in my hands, and I cried.

After a few minutes, I heard Dad yell "Emma, dinner!" I got up and made my way back to the house, the fresh moonlight and the very last bit of sun lighting our way. When I got to the house, I looked through the window to see my parents laughing and setting the table for dinner. I quietly opened the door and was struck again by the warmth and inviting aromas from the kitchen.

My face was damp and blotchy from crying; a trait I inherited from my mother. Someone could always tell when we were crying-even hours after the fact.

"Hey, what's wrong, honey?" my momma asked, reaching to give me a hug.

I tried to manage my emotions, but I walked to her and fell into her arms and started to weep. I felt my dad's comforting hand on my back. I pushed gently away from my mother's embrace and stepped back so I could see both of them. They were searching my eyes for answers so I wiped my tears so I could see them as clearly as I could.

"Momma, I need to tell you something, but I'm afraid you are going to be upset," I struggled to maintain my composure.

"What is it honey? You know you can tell us anything," she said earnestly.

"Whatever it is, it will be okay," Dad echoed.

I took a deep breath, lifted my chin as high as I could manage and told them what my heart had been telling me ever since the summer day that had changed my life forever.

"I want to give Ophelia away. I want to give away my horse."

Chapter 2

The New Girl
(Several Months Earlier)

Summer was approaching and everyone at Hound Hollow was looking forward to the warmer days. Horse shows, trail rides, and new horses moving in were just a few of the reasons to be excited. Stephen and I had become close friends, and Cadence had remained a role model for me at the barn. Miss Natalie was one for giving group lessons and she had trained us together throughout the spring. We had become quite comfortable with our weekly sessions and we had even gotten a little protective of our time together. After our lesson every week, we would hang out in the barn and talk while we cleaned our tack and did barn chores. I was no longer the youngest kid in the barn; my list of responsibilities was growing, and Miss Natalie had even started asking me to get on the sale horses. That was huge for me because it was a sign of her trust and that she thought my skill set was growing. I don't know how Ophelia felt about me riding other horses and I often wondered about it. If she did mind, she certainly didn't take it out on me when I rode her. In fact, she had become a much better horse under saddle as well as in the barn. She'd blossomed under the care at Hound Hollow and had changed from a common chestnut mare to a horse of considerable substance. She had filled out everywhere and was often complimented on her lovely doe eyes and beautiful, shiny coat. I was so proud of her and everything we had accomplished together. We even won some of the better competitions, which was something that I had dreamed of but really didn't expect; especially considering the way we had started out.

This particular day, we were getting ready to have our lesson when an unfamiliar car pulled into the driveway. A girl my age got out of the passenger side. She was pretty and lightly made. She seemed as though she had been around horses quite a bit, judging by the way she was dressed. Stephen, Cadence, and I looked out the window of the tack room and then shared a look. "Who is that?" Cadence inquired.

"Not a clue." Stephen replied, "She must be new."

Miss Natalie came across the stone driveway and gave the driver of the car a long hug, which was quite out of character for her and made us even more interested in the stranger. They spoke briefly before Natalie turned and shook the girl's hand. She held a saddle against her left hip and her helmet was already on her head. Her hair was done perfectly; her hairnet held her hair halfway across her ear with no sign of loose strands anywhere. She had small pearl earrings, polished tall boots, and brown schooling breeches that fit her snugly. Her face was round and soft, with large blue eyes that were kind and inviting. Her expressions with Miss Natalie were confident, almost businesslike. I felt threatened by her presence, even though there seemed to be nothing at all wrong with her. Perhaps that is why I felt that way; she seemed *too* perfect. Stephen seemed particularly interested in her. He didn't notice he'd dropped his tack sponge on the floor as he continued to stare out the window; pretending he was still cleaning his tack.

"Are you okay there, Stephen?" Cadence teased as she winked at me.

Stephen blushed and tried to hold back a smile. We laughed together, but fell quiet as the tack room door opened. The girl in question came in, followed by Miss Natalie.

"Stephen, Cadence, Emma, this is Hailey."

We all gave a polite "hello", while Stephen made the effort to reach out and shake her hand.

"It's nice to meet you, Hailey," Stephen said straight away. He was very forward and looked right at her, just as he did with me when we had met a couple years prior.

"It is nice to meet all of you too." Hailey replied, "I hope you are all right with me joining your lesson today."

I glanced at Miss Natalie with a puzzled face and she corrected me with a stern look.

"Yes," Miss Natalie announced before we could respond, "Hailey will be joining your group today. She will be riding Tigger, the new little dark bay in the end stall."

"Emma," Miss Natalie began as she walked out of the tack room, "would you please show Hailey where everything is? I want to see you all in the tack in thirty minutes."

Before I had the chance to respond, Hailey was already thanking me for helping.

"I really appreciate it, thank you Emma."

"Sure, no problem," I responded. I was polite, but still suspicious. She seemed to come out of nowhere. I didn't say much, just enough to show her where the tack was and where Tigger was stabled.

"Thanks again," she said sweetly. "I can take it from here. I don't want to hold you up."

"Sure thing," I responded quickly as I turned back to get Ophelia out of her stall to tack her up.

"Hey girl," I greeted Ophelia as I approached her stall. When I slid the door open she turned to me, her ears pricked forward as if she were happy to see me and also, quite eager for a treat.

I reached into my pocket for a sugar cube when I heard a bucket bang in the stall next to her. I looked over but I couldn't see a horse in it. I quickly closed Ophelia's door so I could investigate. I went over to the stall and looked down to find a fat, gray, happy welsh pony gorging on her hay. It must have been the new pony, Roxy. She had been a legendary show pony in Maryland before spending time in lesson barns teaching beginners to ride. I had heard that a local girl had gotten her and was coming to Hound Hollow to ride with Natalie. The pony's eyes were sweet and a deep black; her eyelashes were also black and were so long they looked almost fake. It gave her the sweetest look that I had ever seen on a pony. I snuck her a sugar cube, which she took gently from my hand. Moments later, she did the oddest thing. She turned her tongue sideways in her mouth and was sucking on it as though she was trying to get the last bit of sugar off the top of her tongue. It was cute and strange all at the same time and it was something that I had never seen a horse do before. Her funny trick went on for several minutes as I tacked up Ophelia.

As I walked out of the barn and headed for the ring, a young girl, who looked to be about nine years old, came bouncing down the aisle from the opposite direction. The sun shone behind her, catching the highlights in her blonde hair. I noticed with heartfelt appreciation the joy in her step. As she neared the stall, she dropped everything in her hands, ran to her pony, and gave her a big hug. The pony put her head over the little girl's shoulder as if to hug her back.

I thought of the little girl as I approached the ring. She reminded me of advice that my dad would give me. He would probably tell me that everyone has a little girl inside them, and that is who we should always look for, because that is where the goodness lies. He would tell me not to judge someone until I knew their story and have walked in their shoes. I decided to change my attitude about Hailey. Once I did get more of her story, I was grateful that I had straightened myself out.

We were all sharp that day. Competition, real or imagined, will do that for a rider, and I suspect that is at least partially what Miss Natalie had in mind. When we were done, she told us to take Hailey for a walk around the perimeter of the farm. Cadence was the first to pry to find out the details of the stranger.

"So, where are you from Hailey? I can tell you have a little bit of an accent, but I'm not sure what it is."

"I'm from Colorado," she replied.

"Bucks County, Pennsylvania is a long way from Colorado. What are you doing here? Did you move or something?"

"I am just here for the summer to help my Aunt Clara and visit my cousin, Charlotte. Charlotte is very sick, and my Aunt Clara must go to the city almost every day to be with her. Charlotte has two younger brothers that I will babysit while she is there. They used to live in Colorado too, and we were really close growing up."

"What is wrong with your cousin?" Stephen asked. "Will she be okay?"

"I hope she'll be okay," Hailey replied wistfully. "She has a rare form of cancer, so they are not really sure what is going on. Right now, we are just hoping for the best and we feel blessed that she is near Philadelphia where there are so many great cancer doctors."

The mood shifted quickly. We were ashamed about our jokes and snap judgment of her. The guilt was nearly palatable.

"I have heard that," said Stephen, and even if he hadn't, it seemed like the right thing to say.

"I hope your cousin is going to be okay," I said.

Cadence nodded softly in agreement as she looked away.

"Thank you," Hailey replied.

I tried to change the subject, not sure at all of what was appropriate because I had never been in a situation like that before.

"So, how did you like Tigger?"

"Oh! He was so much fun!" She replied cheerfully. "This is your mare, Ophelia, right? She seems really nice too."

"She is," I replied. "I love her. She is the best horse for me, that is for sure."

When we returned to the barn, everyone went their own way to care for their horse. We ended up at the tack room at the end of the night. It was quiet for the most part, until my mom pulled in the drive to pick me up. Hailey's aunt was right behind her, and when they got out of their cars they started to chat.

"It looks like we might be here a while longer," Hailey sighed. "Once my Aunt Clara gets talking, it can be difficult to stop her."

"Oh my gosh, my mom can be the same way!"

We started to talk about school and about the barn where she rides in Colorado.

"What is the name of the farm back home where you ride?" I asked.

"Oh, I ride at–" Just then the door opened and my mom, her Aunt Clara, and Miss Natalie came into the tack room.

"Hi Momma!" I exclaimed.

"Hi sweetheart. How was Ophelia?"

"She was perfect!"

Miss Natalie handled the introductions.

"Yes," my mom said, "we were chatting outside. It turns out that Clara and I know a lot of the same people."

"Clara, really, I hope you take me up on my offer. I would be more than happy to help in any way I can. My schedule is very flexible during the day. Anytime you need me to drive Hailey to the barn or help with the boys, please give me a holler."

"I just may take you up on that. Thank you so much. I am really glad I ran into you."

"Sure thing!" My mom replied as she turned to me. "Emma, how about you? Are you all set to go?"

"Yes, Momma, I just want to give Ophelia one more squeeze before we leave."

"Okay, honey. I will meet you in the car. Just a quick hug, right?"

"Yes, Momma."

She shot me a coy smile and I smiled back, knowing she is right - I always ended up dwelling and spending as much time at the barn as I could. There is just something about the farm that always makes me feel warm and content. It is not just *one* thing. It is the sound that the horses make when they are eating their hay on a quiet night. It is the mixture of all the smells from the horse's hair, the bedding, the sweet grains and the bridle leather. It is the feeling of being so close to them when grooming and having their full trust when I am on their back. It is their acceptance of me; never being judged, and always feeling as though I am good enough for them. Why would anyone ever want to leave that any sooner than they absolutely had to?

Chapter 3

Fireflies and Bats

Hailey and I became fast friends despite our awkward beginning. We started spending more time together at the barn and I even let her ride Ophelia a few times. I probably wouldn't have if it weren't for Miss Natalie letting me school the sale horses for her. I didn't feel as though I had to be selfish with Ophelia since I was getting to experience so many other horses. I was, however, a little taken aback at how well Ophelia went for Hailey. Miss Natalie sensed this and made it a point to mention that it was a result of the work I had done with her. This put me at ease, plus I could tell that Hailey was thrilled to get on a horse other than the school horses, and that made me feel good for her.

A long, wet spring made for a lush beginning of summer. The leaves on the trees were especially green and rich with life, and as the June heat began to wash over Bucks County, they provided much needed cover from the searing sun. Cadence, Hailey, Stephen, and I took the horses on the trails around Hound Hollow whenever we could. Miss Natalie said it was good to get the horses fit out in the country and it prevented them from getting sour from too much time in the ring. Neither reason mattered to us; it felt natural and right to be out of doors with the horses and the day was always measured in terms of joy. We had the time, or so it seemed, to go on these rides forever. We never worried about anything when we rode out together. There was so much to love that kept us captive in our perfect world; the sweat soaked horses with creek water dripping off their bellies, the smell of the sweet corn and honeysuckle filling our noses, and the harmonious sound of our laughter that complimented the hoof beats that struck the earth in a constant, flawless rhythm. The setting sun would light our way home and paint the sky in magnificence to give us something to admire at the end of our day. There was also the occasional shower that would come out of a passing cloud that would sprinkle just enough rain to cool us off and keep the dust of the trail down. Then, there were the trees. They were always such a mystery to me. I wondered why they would go through the effort to generously envelop us in a splendorous cover from a scorching sun and then all but abandon us in just a few months' time. I know that I would see them back in their full, perfect form one day, but I wondered, why did they have to leave us at all? Regardless, beneath it all I sensed a perfection that I couldn't define and that I never wanted to leave.

Cadence was the oldest of us and was heading off to University the following year. She was the only one that seemed to drift past the moment that we were all living in. She wouldn't say anything in particular, but we could sense her uncertainty. The uncertainty, I believe, of what it meant to actually grow up.

One Saturday, in lieu of our trail ride, I asked Hailey if she would like to come to my house. It was the first time I had done so and she agreed readily as she had been spending so much time watching her younger cousins that she was eager for a change. The boys were going to the city to spend time with their sister Charlotte because she had a 'big procedure' coming up, as Hailey called it, and her Aunt Clara thought it was important for the boys to spend time with her. This left Hailey open for the rest of the afternoon and evening, so we planned for her to come to Wycombe and spend the night.

My mom came to the farm to drive us back to the house. She seemed as excited for the sleepover as we were and Daddy was planning a special dinner for us. I just wanted Hailey to feel comfortable, because I knew how it felt to sleep someplace new. She seemed content though, and I was so pleased to have a friend to show my world to.

Duke and Daddy greeted us straight away when we arrived. Duke went straight to Hailey, jumping towards her and bracing his front paws on her forearm to get as close to her as he could. He slid quickly to the ground as my Dad corrected him sharply, albeit with a smile, seeing that Hailey was fine with the intrusion.

"Duke! Down!"

"It's okay Mr. Sterling, we have two dogs back home. I'm used to it. Oh, he is *so* cute!" Hailey squealed, getting down on one knee while Duke lavished her with kisses.

"Is it okay if we take Duke for a walk?" I asked. "Are you up for that, Hailey?"

"Oh, yes, for sure!"

"Sure Emma girl, we will eat around six," my Dad replied in that special tone that made everything feel just right.

We set off across the yard to the hedgerow of trees that bordered the cornfield. The corn was not quite past our waists, so Mom and Dad could see us all the way to the very edge of the field until the woods. I looked back on occasion and I could see my dad pretending to do something important in the yard, but I knew he was just keeping watch. I loved that about my daddy. I loved that he let me go on adventures, but still wanted to be there to protect me. Duke hurried along in front as if he was anxious to show Hailey all of his favorite haunts. We headed straight for the creek so we could cool off. We worked our way carefully down a steep hill to the edge of the water. Duke splashed in without hesitation while the two of us mixed giggles with shrieks as we dipped our feet in the water. We waded through the clear stream, bending down to examine the effulgent rocks of various colors, screeching riotously as crayfish sped quickly to the safety of another stone, seeming to vanish into another world beneath our feet and beyond our sight.

"Let's explore the woods!" Hailey exclaimed. The sun shined through the trees and on to the droplets of creek water on her arms and face, making her sparkle like she was covered in crystals.

"Okay!" I replied, "Duke, come!"

Duke reluctantly left the cool water and followed us through the woods as Hailey led the way. We came upon a spot that looked as though it had been made just for us. It was at the edge of a grove of pine trees and had big boulders, one of which was shaped like a chair. It was partially covered with moss and dirt, but it was such a wonderful spot that we took turns sitting in it, while the other sat on a fallen ash tree that looked as though it just recently separated itself from its century long relationship with the earth.

Duke was obsessively sniffing at a spot about halfway down the length of the tree right at a point where a massive limb connected to the trunk. He started digging, dirt flying under his belly and into the air. Hailey and I got up to investigate. Lodged under the tree was an old metal box. We grabbed sturdy sticks and helped Duke dig until we were able to pull it free. We slid the latch and opened it in anticipation, but to our disappointment it was empty.

"What do you think it's from?" Hailey asked.

"I have no idea, but I bet someone else used to spend time here. Maybe they used it to keep secrets?" I said mysteriously.

"Maybe." Hailey replied hopefully. "What do you think we should do with it? Maybe we should keep it here. We can come here whenever we want this summer, and we can put things in it. I don't know what, but we can use it like one of those time capsules that people put things in and open it years later."

We let our imaginations run about how it had gotten there. It was just an old, metal box, but for some reason it held our attention in a way I couldn't explain. We agreed to leave it and to make the whole area our secret hiding place that we could come to throughout the summer during her visit. For now, the box would remain empty.

We made our way back in plenty of time for dinner. Daddy made barbeque chicken and sweet corn on the grill. We sat and ate cheerfully with my parents at a picnic table that my dad had made over the winter in his workshop. After supper, I showed Hailey around our house. I always liked to show people our home because it seemed as though I was the only person they would know that lived in such an old house, and the Victorian features made it unique, offering something that other, newer houses couldn't. While our home was different and intriguing, it was also very old. With old houses came things that could make people uneasy. Old pipes would make faint creaking sounds like footsteps that would travel from the basement to the third floor; creating frightening notions of unwanted company in the imagination.

I had moved my room to the third floor that past spring, giving my parents the whole second floor to themselves. We had two spare rooms on the third floor, so I showed Hailey where she could sleep. She chose the room that my mom called the "wedding room." Its walls were covered in pictures from both sides of my family and of weddings past. The walls were a dark Victorian rose color. The white lace curtains, which

25

matched the canopy bed, glowed faintly; reflecting the light of the small, single electric candle that Mom kept lit in the window all year long. I told Hailey it was okay if she left it on while she slept. I always did. I am not sure if it was because I was just a touch afraid of the dark or because I was reassured by the light, but regardless, I wanted to give my friend the feeling of knowing where to put her feet should she wake in the night.

After the tour, we went downstairs to sit on the porch. Hailey swayed on the porch swing while I sat on the railing, both awestruck as fireflies took over the sky after the sun had set. We looked on in childish wonderment as they lit their tiny bodies simultaneously, as though they were sending some sort of secret message to one another. Whatever the message, it gave me a feeling of peace and tranquility, until a shriek exploded from Hailey, which nearly made me fall off the porch railing, my heart pounding wildly in my chest.

"A bat!" she screeched, running towards me, grabbing my arm for security.

"Oh, gosh Hailey. Yes, it was a bat. There are lots of them," I said reassuringly, not realizing that wouldn't help at all.

"*Lots* of them?" she asked, her voice shaking.

Hearing Hailey's screech, Mom and Dad rushed to the porch. "What's wrong, girls? What happened?"

"Hailey saw a bat, and it scared her."

"I'm sorry Mrs. Sterling. I had never seen one that close before."

My parents smiled reassuringly at Hailey, and we all started to giggle.

"There is nothing to worry about, Hailey," my dad explained sympathetically. "They come out of that house across the street. They live in the belfry and they show up every summer. They eat the mosquitos; I can assure you they have no interest in you or Emma."

We looked out at the yard as Hailey sighed with relief. We watched as the bats dove for their food and the fireflies did their part in illuminating the night sky, sometimes so much so that you could catch a glimpse of the tiny bat face, which looked demonic compared to the innocent, bright bugs.

"What about the fireflies? Do the bats eat them?"

"No, they don't," my mom informed Hailey, "They actually have no interest in them at all."

"That's good. But why not?" she asked, "I would think they would be easy for a bat to catch."

"The firefly's light is toxic to a bat. If they eat them, they can get sick and even die."

Hailey paused and looked out at the yard again, this time with a little less apprehension.

"You girls head to bed soon," my mom encouraged, "I bet you have a big day planned tomorrow."

"Okay Momma."

"Good night Mrs. Sterling. Good night Mr. Sterling," Hailey said sweetly.

"Good night Hailey, good night Emma girl."

"Good night Momma, good night Daddy."

Not long after, Hailey and I went upstairs to go to bed. She wasn't in her room long enough for me to lie down before she knocked on my door.

"Emma, can I come in?"

"Sure, what's up?"

"I am kinda scared. Can I sleep on your floor?"

"Yes, of course! Let's grab the blankets from your bed."

We set up a spot for Hailey, then I pulled the blankets off my bed so we both could lie on the floor, looking up at the shadows on the ceiling, still talking, but slower and slower as we neared unconsciousness. Just before I fell completely asleep, Hailey confessed something that broke my heart.

"I think my cousin is dying. You know, Charlotte."

I wasn't sure what to say, so I said what I thought people say in this situation. Even though it felt like a cliché, I meant it; I felt terrible for her.

"I am so sorry."

I bit my lip nervously, waiting to hear a reply. Nothing came, so I asked a question that I wasn't sure I should ask.

"What exactly is wrong with her?"

Hailey answered without hesitation. "Cancer. She has brain cancer."

"That is awful. I am so sorry, Hailey."

"It's okay. It's just…we were best friends growing up. We did everything together and now she is so sick. I have only been to see her twice since I have been here. I am afraid to go see her, even though I know I should."

Her voice cracked, and she started to sob. "I just don't know what to say to her. I can't stand to see her in that hospital bed. I know she knows I look at her differently and I don't want her to see me pity her. I am just so scared for her."

I remembered back to the trailer accident when I was so afraid to stay with Ophelia. The awful terror of that night stuck with me, but I remembered what my mom told me. She told me that Ophelia needed me to be strong for her. I wasn't sure what to say to Hailey, so I told her the same thing Mom told me that night.

"Do you really think she wants me there?"

"I do. I really do."

"Would you…" Hailey hesitated, "would you go with me? Maybe just once?"

"Sure, I'd be happy to. Especially if it would make you feel better."

"Thank you, Emma. That would mean so much to me. Plus, I really want you to meet her. She is so much fun! She has always been one of my favorite people."

"Sure thing," a long, genuine yawn coming out along with my reply.

After that, we stayed quiet, as did the mysterious noises of the house. A cool, light breeze came through the windows and washed over us as we drifted off to sleep, listening to the sound of crickets chirping happily in the night.

Chapter 4

I am Charlotte

Driving through the city to get to the University hospital left me with a feeling of general unease that bordered, at times, on anxiousness. The rain hitting our windshield with a melancholy rhythm kept us quiet.

"I think this is the longest I have ever heard you two sit quietly together," my mom quipped; I think, in an effort to break what was becoming an uncomfortable silence.

"I'm sorry Mrs. Sterling, I guess the rain is making me tired," Hailey said apologetically, her gaze fixed out the window, her head and neck tilted awkwardly upward at the skyscrapers that stretched ominously towards the sunless sky.

My anxiety increased as we searched for a parking space; I wasn't used to the intensity of the city traffic. It wasn't that I didn't like the city; I just couldn't keep up with everything that was happening around me, which left me feeling unsettled.

We ended up in a parking garage; our three car doors echoed vacantly as they slammed shut, followed by the lock of the door, which was another unusual sound to me as we never bothered to lock our doors in the country. We made our way through the sterile matrix of the hospital to Charlotte's room. The hospital was brighter and more inviting than what I had expected; it was intentionally colorful and modern, which gave me a sense of hope despite my uncertainty. We passed so many children, some my age, dressed in hospital gowns; some whom had IVs and monitors hooked up to them. I tried not to stare but it was hard not to as I hesitantly processed things that I had never before witnessed.

I was relieved to reach Charlotte's room. Just before we entered, Hailey gently pulled me aside.

"Emma, just one thing…"

"Sure, what is it?"

"It might be hard but try to act as normal as you can."

"Sure, of course," I replied reassuringly but with very little confidence.

I was overwhelmed with a sadness that I had never experienced before. As we stood there together, I was frozen; entranced by the busy nurses rushing about, unaffected by the despair that surrounded them.

"Girls, I will wait out here," my mom said in a comforting tone, "take as much time as you want."

"Are you ready to meet Charlotte?" Hailey asked me cheerfully.

"Yes," I replied as Hailey led the way into the room.

"Oh my gosh!" Charlotte shrilled when she saw Hailey, stretching her arms eagerly towards her.

Hailey gave her cousin a long hug that brightened the mood immediately. As Hailey straightened up, a copy of "The Secret Garden" slid off of Charlotte's bed and onto the floor, so I quickly reached for it to hand it back to her.

"Thank you! That is my favorite book," she said cheerfully.

"Sure, I am Emma, Hailey's friend," I replied as I gently handed the book back to her.

"I am Charlotte," she said, fixing her eyes on mine; exuding a soft confidence that surprised me.

"Hi," I squeaked, very aware of how nervous I sounded. I didn't want her to know I was uncomfortable in the hospital, but the more I tried to sound normal, the harder it was. I felt flush.

"It's nice to meet you, Emma," she continued, her pale face full of hope and happiness. I looked into her large, brown eyes, fascinated by how beautiful she was despite her head being covered by a purple bandana and a plain, cold looking hospital gown as her top. Her room was decorated with pictures, flowers, and dozens of cards. Despite all of the well wishes, it hardly seemed enough to comfort anyone, but Charlotte seemed unfazed. Oddly enough, she only seemed to care about Hailey and me.

Charlotte continued to watch me intently, "I have heard so much about you! I heard you ride horses. I have always wanted to ride. You have your own horse, right?"

"Yes, yes," I stuttered. "Her name is Ophelia."

"What a pretty name!"

"Thank you, yes, I love her."

Hailey and I sat down in chairs next to Charlotte's bed. After Hailey and Charlotte caught up a while, Charlotte pointed at a cabinet in the corner of the room that had about a dozen board games stacked neatly together.

"Do you want to play a game?" she asked.

"Sure, that would be fun," Hailey answered, "what do you want to play?"

"You pick!" she exclaimed.

We settled in and spent the next two hours joking and talking; I mostly listened as they reminisced about their childhood. I found myself admiring the bond they shared, as it seemed so genuine and rare.

Mom gently knocked on the open door and told us it was time to make our way home. As uncomfortable as I was at the beginning of the visit, I found myself reluctant to leave.

After introducing my mom to Charlotte, we got up to go. Charlotte offered Hailey and me long, tender hugs.

"Please say you will come back soon," she pleaded, including me in her hopeful look. "Or hopefully I can get out of here and come visit you. I would love to meet your horse, Emma!"

"Yes, that would be great. I would really like that," I agreed.

We left the room slowly, leaving my new friend beaming behind us.

Chapter 5

Best Friends - The Three of Us

On our drive home from the hospital, Hailey and I promised one another that we would go back and visit Charlotte as often as we could through the summer. Hailey was set to go home in the middle of August, when the Colorado schools started back up, so we wanted to take advantage of every day that we had together. She continued taking care of Charlotte's little brothers when her Aunt Clara and Uncle David were with Charlotte, but the rest of the time we were inseparable; we were either at Hound Hollow or at my house, and we even spent two days away with my parents at Rehoboth beach. The trail rides we took together through the woods were the best part. Miss Natalie had me ride the sale horses to get them used to trails, so one day I offered to let Hailey ride Ophelia. Ophelia had become so well behaved out in the country that she was the perfect companion for the young and green stock that I got to ride. I loved watching Ophelia with Hailey together, and I could tell that Ophelia liked Hailey very much.

It had rained torrentially the night before, so we had to tread carefully, using the high areas to make our way down to the creek where we intended to cross to get to a grove of pines that we liked to maneuver through; teaching our horses to bend and turn while weaving through the tall, alluring forest. I was on a handsome, gray gelding. The seven-year-old Dutch bred horse was named "Illusion", and he was at Miss Natalie's to be sold as a show jumper. His mane was nearly black in contrast to his light gray coat, which had dapples of darker gray that spread out over his back and sides. He was a lovely horse; the kind that everyone wanted to help train.

We were quiet as we let our horses work their way towards our destination; we were filled with worry for Charlotte. She looked well the day prior, when we visited, but she had another big surgery coming up that was more complex than the previous one. She didn't give us details, but we could tell by her expression that she was scared.

Hailey broke the silence on the subject. "Do you think Charlotte will be okay? I mean, with the surgery."

I wanted to stay positive. "Yes, I am sure of it, Hailey. My mom said they have the best doctors in the world here working with her."

"I'm so worried about her. I don't know what to say when she tells me about stuff like that."

"I think that just being there is enough. You've gotten to spend so much time with her this summer and I can tell she appreciates it."

"Yes, I know, which is all thanks to you and your mom. I am so grateful that you went with me that first day and that your mom has been willing to drive to the city so often. Not everyone would do that for someone they just met."

Our talk got us to the base of the stream, which looked more like a river after all the recent rainfall. The horse's feet started to sink in the mud as we neared the edge, causing them to struggle and panic a bit, so we pulled them both back a few steps to assess the situation. The water was higher and rushing more than I had ever seen it at our crossing spot. We could usually see the bottom, even in the deep areas that came to the horse's chest, but on this day, it was dark and hard to see anything but the water's edge. Hailey and I looked at one another, shrugged, and giggled.

"You first?" I suggested playfully. "You are on the more experienced horse," I continued, "I thought they had bigger streams in Colorado than Pennsylvania. This should be easy for you."

Hailey turned straight away with a smile and urged Ophelia towards the water. Illusion and I followed close behind. The water was soon up to the bottom of our boots, providing the horses relief from the miles of trails under the searing July sun.

We were fine the first few feet in, but then the strong current caused the horses to move sideways with the flow of the water, setting us off target for crossing to the other side. Hailey was struggling to keep Ophelia straight when suddenly she shrieked in fear.

"Emma! What's happening?"

The current had pushed them down towards a deep spot in the creek. I watched in astonishment as Ophelia's body nearly disappeared, her head and neck raised upward to keep her mouth and nose free from the water.

"Emma!" She shouted, "What do I do? What do I do? Help!"

I couldn't answer, as I was trying to steady my own horse. Illusion started to lose his footing on the slippery rocks hidden by the rushing waters. I pushed him hard with my left leg to prevent him from drifting towards Ophelia. It wasn't working; I started to panic! I looked over my shoulder to see if I could turn back to the bank, but it was too late. I was stuck, so I had no choice but to commit to getting across.

Hailey screamed again, "Emma! Help! What do I do?"

As she spoke, I felt Illusion's body start to change completely underneath of me. I had never felt this sensation before, but then I realized what it was; we were swimming! In a moment my feeling went from absolute terror to an immeasurable bliss.

"Oh my gosh, we're swimming!" I yelled to Hailey.

"What do I do?" Hailey yelped, not nearly as enamored with the moment as I was.

"She looks happy!" I exclaimed. "You're okay. The horses aren't scared, and they know what to do. Just work your way down stream to the shallow part and go up the bank."

I squealed with laughter as the water soaked my waist. Hailey finally started to relax and she laughed along with me.

"We're swimming! I can't believe this!" she exclaimed.

We managed to make our way to the shallow water downstream where I had never crossed horses before. Fortunately, the bank was low, so we were able to make our way up it and into the forest. We made our way towards the vast collection of pines, where we looked at one another and burst out laughing.

Ophelia looked refreshed; her coat a brilliant copper under the sunshine, her mane glistening with a million shades of red. I smiled as Hailey reached down and hugged Ophelia's neck with a sweet affection that could only be found in a pure moment without thought. I remembered the day when I had fallen from Ophelia and how she had come back to me instead of running to the barn. What she did that day for me was immeasurable, and now it seemed she was doing the same for Hailey, but in a different way. I think she could tell Hailey was deeply sad, and she was doing everything she could to make her happy. In that moment, I felt so proud of who Ophelia had become and everything that we had done together, that I started to get emotional. Hailey spotted a tear that had worked its way to the corner of my eye.

"Are you okay?"

"Yes, just perfect. Everything is perfect."

"Okay, good! Are you ready to show me this forest?"

"Yes! Let's do this, but when we head back, we should probably find a shallower place to cross the creek!"

"Agreed!" Hailey replied, laughing with me as we worked our way into the calmness of the magnificent forest ahead of us.

◆ ◆ ◆

It was just past lunchtime as we reached the barn. Hailey and I simultaneously recognized a familiar figure in the distance that whipped us into a frenzy.

"Is that...?" I stammered.

"It is! It's Charlotte!"

We urged Illusion and Ophelia into a trot down the tractor path towards our friend, who was standing with her mom and little brothers.

"This is so exciting! What are you doing here?" Hailey asked happily.

"The doctors said I could get out some this week and I wanted to spend time with you and Emma. I can't ride, but I can do other things, as long as I take it easy."

Hailey and I traded a glance, knowing right away where we needed to take our friend.

"Great!" I exclaimed, "Ms. Clara, is it okay if Charlotte helps us give the horses a bath? Ophelia is really safe and quiet."

"I suppose, just be really careful, okay? I will play outside with the boys until you are done. I spoke with your mom, Emma, and we planned a sleepover for the three of you at your house tonight."

We all yelped delightedly at the thought. Hailey and I jumped off our mounts and led Charlotte into the barn.

"So, what do you guys want to do?" asked Charlotte.

"Whatever you want," I replied.

Hailey echoed the sentiment.

"Let's just do whatever it is you normally do when you are together. That would be perfect."

Hailey and I beamed. Hailey had quickly become as infatuated with our house and the property around it as I had always been, and just as my mom had been when she was a child.

"We have a secret spot to show you and so many stories to tell you," I exclaimed. "My dad will cook whatever you want on the grill and we can stay up as late as you like."

"This already sounds great!" she exclaimed.

I soaked Ophelia in soap and covered her in bubbles from her hooves to her ears. I handed Charlotte the hose and instructed her to start rinsing Ophelia by first hosing her legs, and then steadily working her way up to her topline and then back down. She seemed to enjoy watching the dirty creek water and sweat rinse from the mare's body to reveal the scarlet perfection underneath. I showed her how to scrape the water off her back, then her sides and then her belly. We finished by drying her legs with a thick cotton towel; careful to make sure her pasterns

44

were extra dry. I handled her back legs for fear that Ophelia might kick at a stray fly and possibly injure Charlotte. Charlotte cautiously crouched down next to the mare and thoroughly dried her front legs. Lastly, I gave her a mane comb to comb the mane flat to the opposite of the mounting side of the horse. Once through, she stepped back and admired Ophelia.

"She is magnificent. Just magnificent," she repeated, awestruck.

When we got home, Duke greeted Charlotte and Hailey with a fervor of kisses as my Dad stood over the hot grill preparing dinner. There was a lovely breeze that gently swept all the humidity out of the air, leaving no resistance to all that was lovely and right. The fireflies would soon be out to brighten the night with their black, nefarious friends diving through the sky at their prey. But first, Hailey and I wanted to take Charlotte to our secret spot in the woods.

"Daddy, we are going to the woods, okay?"

"What about dinner, Emma? Aren't you hungry?"

"Ooh Daddy, can we please take it with us?"

"Sure, I don't see why not. Go grab the picnic basket out of the dining room closet and I will set you girls right up!"

We all chimed in with a series of thanks to my dad and headed out. As we were leaving, he teasingly reminded us, "Be careful-and remember to watch out for the Indian man!"

"Stop it, Daddy!" I chided, "Don't freak us out before we go in the woods!"

"Who is the 'Indian man'?" asked Charlotte.

"Oh, it's just a silly story my Dad likes to tell. I betcha we'll hear that story later tonight!"

Duke, smelling the food that Daddy had packed for us, followed close behind. The corn was tall now that it was late July. It reached well over our heads, so we felt as though we were miles away as soon as we stepped out of our yard. We made our way to the woods noisily, Duke's collar jingling, the cornstalks brushing our sides, and infectiously cackling laughter that none of us could stop. We worked our way down the bank to our secret spot, and invited Charlotte to sit in the honorary 'chair' made of rock while Hailey and I found comfy spots on the fallen tree trunk. We ate our dinner of hot dogs and macaroni salad while Duke looked on intently, waiting for us to drop a morsel or two.

When we were done eating, I went to the hollow of the tree and pulled out the metal box that had turned into a treasure chest for Hailey and me. I handed it to Charlotte, and she opened it carefully; she seemed as intrigued as Hailey and I had been with the simple but mysterious container. She placed it on her lap and sorted through the contents. There were our diaries, along with some of the prettiest rocks that we had found while creek walking. Besides our secrets and our stones, we kept anything we had found on the forest floor that held our interest. We had teeth from a deer skull, a rusty pocketknife that Hailey had found in the crotch of an old oak tree, and several old medicine bottles of different colors. Charlotte was fascinated by our finds. After we went over each item in detail, we decided to make our way home. I carefully placed the box back in its safe spot before we left.

"Can we take the long way back?" Charlotte asked. "So I can see more of the forest?"

"Sure!" Hailey and I answered together. "Whatever you want. It is *your* day, Charlotte."

We did take the long way back, as Charlotte requested, working our way through the cornfield while giggling and sometimes even snorting with laughter. We talked about boys, school, horses, and everything else that was fun and wonderful in our world. Pushing through the last few rows of stalks, we burst onto the lawn. We were greeted by the glow of a small fire, and my parents sitting nearby, with three chairs ready for us to join them.

"This is so much fun!" Charlotte said thankfully to my parents, smiling broadly while trying to catch her breath.

"Of course, Charlotte! You are more than welcome. We are so glad you are here."

My mom had a table set up for s'mores and my dad had already carved sticks for marshmallows, so we sat and made our treats while my mom and dad sipped their drinks and smiled tenderly at us. For a moment that no one else noticed, I paused and gazed at my parents. I soaked in their faces as the fire flickered flames of bright yellows and blue that gave their skin a sweet glow. I could tell they were in love more than I had ever seen them. This pleased me so much and I felt complete as I looked at them, and at my friends on either side of me. We all sat quietly for a spell until my dad broke the silence.

"So, did Emma tell you girls about the Indian man?"

"Daddy, you never really told me the whole story. What is your obsession?" I questioned, rolling my eyes and smiling at him.

"Well, it is a true story; in fact, your mom told it to me the very first time I came here."

The fire caught the essence of Dad's handsome, kind face as he told his story in boy-like fashion. We leaned forward, listening intently to his tale.

"You see, when Emma's mom, Julia, was a little girl living in this house, one summer night just like this, she looked out her bedroom window – the room that is now Emma's – and swore she saw the figure of a man dressed like an Indian. His back was to her and he seemed to be watching the old farmhouse across the street."

"You mean the house with all of the bats?" Hailey asked nervously.

"Yes, that one," my Dad replied.

"Anyway, she was so convinced of what she had seen that she woke her parents up. Alarmed, they called the police, but they searched the whole property and they didn't find anyone, so it was dismissed as nothing but shadows or Julia's imagination."

"Years later though, your mom had a friend who had the ability to feel the presence of ghosts. Sitting out on the porch with a group of friends one night, entirely unprompted, the woman said she felt the presence of a man dressed like an Indian, headdress and all, standing at that very spot."

We shuffled nervously in our chairs and leaned in even closer as Dad continued.

"Years later, when new neighbors bought the old farmhouse, they researched the property; the deed showed a family from a local Indian tribe name had owned it. What we think happened is that when the owners after him stopped caring for the property and let it fall to ruin, he couldn't take it. So instead, he left, moving across the street to our property to watch over it from afar.

He stands right by the old white pines, probably so he can shelter under them when it rains."

"Do you think that is why I get the creeps every time I go past that spot?" I asked.

"Yikes, *I* just got chills." Hailey whispered, Charlotte nodded in agreement, and they shuddered.

"Anyway, I will leave you girls with that. Emma, just let me know when you come in for the night and I will put the fire out."

"Okay Daddy. Thank you for everything."

The girls grinned and thanked him too.

"Do you think any of that was true?" Charlotte whispered after my parents had gone inside.

"Oh, I don't know for sure. He does sound convincing though, doesn't he?" I answered.

"I just, I just..." Charlotte stuttered softly.

"What is it Charlotte?" Hailey asked, sensing a change in Charlotte's mood.

"I just think, if it's true, how sad the Indian man must be. If a house that I loved that much was destroyed like his, I think I would do the same thing. I would want to leave it so I wouldn't have to dwell there, suffering while it was being ruined for no good reason. Then, if I could, I imagine I would stand by just close enough to see if somehow, someway, it could ever be fixed and be made whole again."

Charlotte stared thoughtfully into the fire, a look of certainty on her face. We all sat quietly until the fire burned low, leaving nothing but the embers keeping the earth aglow. We made our way into the house, and after I said good night to my parents, I led the way to the third floor. We decided to pull the covers off the beds and put them on the floor for a proper slumber party. I had a small battery powered lamp that I put between us. Charlotte started telling jokes and Hailey and I followed. The next thing we knew we were are laughing uncontrollably, even at the slightest sound we would make; our eyes filled with laughter-tears that slipped down our cheeks. We eventually laid our heads down to sleep, and as we did, Charlotte spoke.

"Thank you for such a wonderful day. I really needed it. I needed everything that you gave me. I felt so alone in the hospital, but now here I am, surrounded by my best friends. That is what we are, aren't we?" she asked, her eyes drifting closed. "We are best friends, the three of us."

"Yes," Hailey replied softly.

"Yes, we are," I assured her, my voice as soft as Hailey's.

And with those words, we all fell fast asleep.

Chapter 6

Visiting Hours

The day for Charlotte's surgery came, leaving Hailey and me stressed into silence at the farm. While everything was perfect from moment to moment, every time I let my thoughts venture towards the future it was full of doubt, which left me feeling terribly anxious. Charlotte, Hailey and I had matching bracelets made at the tack shop the week prior. I reached down and ran my fingers across the face of mine, saying a prayer for Charlotte as I did. I went through the motions at the barn; each horse I rode momentarily distracting me from my worries. Miss Natalie could sense our moods, and as usual knew just what to do. She called us into her office and told Hailey, Stephen, Cadence, and me that we were going to have a surprise group lesson.

"Who do you want me on?" Cadence asked, hoping she would have her pick.

"You can ride Tigger. Stephen, of course, will be on Doc, and Emma on Ophelia. Hailey, you ride Illusion. Now get going. You have twenty minutes to be in the tack and your boots better be polished!"

We made our way to our horses and prepared them in military fashion. Everything had to be just right for a Miss Natalie lesson; polished boots, clean bits, and supple, conditioned tack. Most importantly, the horses needed to shine. We rubbed them until the oil from their skin came through their coats and made their hair radiate light.

We had been taking a break from competing this summer to focus on, as Miss Natalie put it, "good, old fashioned horse training." The lessons she gave us were challenging and creative, and today was no exception. After warm-up, we worked for fifteen minutes without stirrups to strengthen our legs, then moved on to a series of jumping grids and finished with course work over fences. When we got to the point of the course work, Miss Natalie had us all halt.

"Okay, let's switch horses. Emma, you get on Illusion, Hailey, you take Ophelia, Stephen, you have Tigger, so that leaves Cadence with Doc."

We dismounted and acquired our new mounts. We switched up our stirrups to our own length and climbed back in the tack to see what Miss Natalie had in store for us.

Without any time to get used to our new mounts she shouted out a ten-jump equitation style course for each of us to complete. I went first and had a terrific course on Illusion, followed by Stephen and Tigger, and then Cadence with Doc, both of whom did equally well. Then it was Hailey's turn. We watched in awe as Hailey stroked flawlessly through the course with Ophelia. I was taken in awe at how well Ophelia jumped for her; they were so slick and accurate with every distance and turn. Ophelia used herself so beautifully that the trip looked flawless.

"Excellent work, everyone! That is plenty for today, don't you think?"

"Yes, Miss Natalie," we chorused, my voice trailing the group, as I was still reeling with astonishment; I wasn't sure whether I should be proud or jealous. Then I saw Hailey reach down and give Ophelia a pat and come back to her position with a huge smile and a tear running down her cheek. With it, a sense of warmth washed over me for my friend that needed to feel something was right in her life. Embarrassed at her show of emotion, Hailey wiped away her tears and blurted, "Who wants to go for a walk around the farm?"

The plan was to ride in the morning and head to the hospital with my dad that evening when Charlotte was out of recovery. Not knowing how long we would be at the farm; Dad had asked Cadence to drive Hailey and me to my house when we were done at Hound Hollow. Cadence stopped her truck and me and Hailey jumped out, running hastily to the porch, waving our thanks as she left. We were excited to get my dad so we could drive into the city to see Charlotte. As we burst through the kitchen door, he was hanging up the phone. My mom had one hand on his arm, the other covering her mouth in a look of shock. They turned towards us, unable to speak. I knew immediately something was wrong.

"Daddy, what is it?"

His face was ashen. "Oh Emma, Emma honey."

I ran towards him. "Daddy, what is it? Is it Charlotte? Is everything okay?"

"Honey, I am so sorry."

My mom reached for Hailey, but she turned and ran out of the house. She took off across the lawn, under the weeping willow tree and towards the woods.

"Hailey!" I yelled, chasing after her.

I found her at our spot, curled up in a ball and crying hysterically while she rocked back and forth. I put my arm around her and held her close, my own tears falling silently, trying my best to stay strong for my friend.

We made our way back to the house together, my arm around her, steadying her against her sorrow. The walk back felt cold and bleak. There were no animals in sight; not a rabbit to flush or a squirrel to scamper up a tree. Even the robins, normally chirring incessantly in the summer dusk, were nowhere to be seen. The tops of the trees stood still with no breeze and the cornstalks, starting to brown, bristled wrathfully against me as I tried in vain to comfort Hailey.

When we got back to the house, Charlotte's mom was waiting in the driveway. Hailey broke from me, giving me a slight squeeze on the arm as she went. She ran to her aunt and collapsed into her arms. They wept together as my parents and I looked on, my mom's arm around me, my dad's arm tight around her. They turned and got in their car without saying anything to us. I watched as Hailey slumped down in her seat. Clara wiped her eyes clear, backed out of the driveway, and left.

The last time I would see Hailey that summer would be a week later at Charlotte's funeral. She left immediately afterwards to return home to

Colorado. She stopped by the barn late at night when no one was around to collect her tack, so when I went to Hound Hollow the day after the funeral, her things were gone. When I walked into the barn that day, it felt as though, for a moment, she had never been there at all.

I went to the board to see my chore list for the day. I didn't have much to say to anyone, so I simply pulled my baseball cap down over my eyes and kept on task. I went to work with vigor for hours, not stopping until the very last stall was cleaned and the last horse groomed. It was odd. I didn't feel sad or angry or anything at all, really. I knew there was work that needed to be done, so I followed the steps and took care of it. I had been that way since the funeral, and if anything, I was more efficient than I had ever been before. I remember realizing how focused I was, and for a moment thought it quite strange that I could be so sharp and productive and void of emotion, given the circumstances that I had endured. Shamefully, I felt proud of myself for being so useful despite everyone mourning around me. It was such an unusual feeling that did not feel right at all, but I couldn't go any deeper or allow myself to feel anything. There was a moment, I think, where I wondered if there could be something wrong with me. I dismissed it and continued to be who I thought everyone needed me to be. I was, at the very least, useful.

I outlasted everyone that day except Natalie, who was outside watering her flowers as the day came to an end. She had only the chore of turning out the horses for the night on her list, which she always saved for last to keep them from the trouble of the summertime bugs feeding on their flesh. I thought momentarily to go speak to her. I sensed I needed someone to talk to, but I wasn't even sure what it was I needed to talk about. I started towards her past my mare's stall, when Ophelia spun around, put her nose up against the stall bars, and looked right at me. She turned her head slightly away from me and blinked softly, her left eye sparkling as it caught the last bit of sun from the day that was coming to an end. I looked at the kind, caring face of my mare, and I burst into tears.

Chapter Seven

Ophelia Understands – She Does!

Every day since the funeral I worked on processing what I had been through. Actually, I tried to process everything *Hailey* had been through. The way I saw it, from the day I met Charlotte, it was never about me at all. She was Hailey's cousin, it was Hailey's trip far from home, Hailey's loss, and her family's loss. I was just someone that was there, a bystander and witness, and while I cared deeply about her and Charlotte, it was Hailey's pain that was profound, not mine.

My parents would check in with me regularly to see how I was doing, and they even had me see a therapist to make sure I was coping the way one should in such a circumstance. There was however, nothing to see and nothing to fix. The truth was, no matter how deep I or anyone else examined myself, I was fine. The trials I had already been through with my Dad and Ophelia prepared me to be strong for Hailey. Somehow, I was ready for what had happened.

◆ ◆ ◆

The night before I told my parents that I wanted to give Ophelia away, I spent most of the day at Hound Hollow. It was a Sunday and Mom had dropped me off right after church. I spent the afternoon working for Miss Natalie, and at the end of the day I took Ophelia out for a hack. We rode the same loop we had the day I fell, but this time she was light and relaxed, with no deer to spook her or storms to worry about. It was just my mare and me, and it was lovely in every way. When we got back to the barn, I took off her tack and gave her a long grooming until her lower lip became droopy and her eyes were soft and half-closed. I gave her a mint and tucked her into her stall. I listened to her peacefully munch her hay while I put my tack away. Exhausted and cold, I curled up on my tack trunk in front of her stall and wrapped myself in her wool blanket. I talked to her as I always did when things were on my mind.

"I hope you can understand me Ophelia. I just don't know what to think anymore. I am so sad for Hailey. I can't imagine going through what she has. She lost so much the day she lost Charlotte. Whenever we talk now, she seems so sad and distant; she only says the bare minimum to me. Even bringing up the good memories hurts. I still have the bracelet that we had made, but I can't bring myself to wear it, so I hid it in our secret box in the woods. I wonder," I hesitated, "I wonder sometimes if there is anything I can do that could *really* help her, that could make her feel good again. Ophelia...I've been thinking: how would you feel if you went to live with Hailey? I love you so much girl, but something deep down inside is telling me I should give you to her."

She lifted her head and stared at me through the bars of the stall, her jaw working on a mouthful of hay, steam coming from her nostrils, clouding the white, imperfect walls of the old bank barn. She put her head back down to continue eating.

"Do you understand at all?"

Miss Natalie startled me as she came up behind me. "Emma, when are your folks coming to get you? It's getting awfully late."

"I'm sorry Miss Natalie, they'll be here any minute, I promise."

"Okay, honey. Make sure you turn off the lights before you leave. Leave the top doors of the stalls open so they can enjoy the fresh air."

"Yes, Ms. Natalie, good night."

"Good night Emma."

I desperately wanted Ophelia to tell me what she was thinking. I had always felt like she understood me, but this was such a big decision, I wished that she could give me a clearer sign. Once Miss Natalie left, the barn was quiet, except for the comforting sounds of the horses chewing their hay and the occasional scurrying of a mouse overhead in the hayloft. I opened Ophelia's stall, and as I stepped through the doorway she stopped eating and nudged me with her nose. I put my arms around her, resting my forehead against her soft neck. Her smell was warm and calming; the sound of her breathing, soothing. With my arms still in place around her, I asked her again, "Ophelia, what do you think I should do? I wish you could tell me."

We sat quietly together until a sense of absolute peace washed over me. Then, I asked her to make me a promise. I asked her to promise me that if I did give her to Hailey, that she would always remember me. I asked that she do the same for Hailey as she had done for me, and that she would stay strong for her forever. I asked that she remember, if she could, all the advice that my mom and Miss Natalie had given us that had helped us through our trials. My voice trembled as I spoke softly to her, and as the last word left my mouth, I felt her body language completely change. She relaxed completely, and wrapped her neck gently around me, and gave me a slow, tender nicker. I pulled away slightly and stared into her eyes. There was no doubt as I gazed at her with my eyes blurry with tears; the nicker that she gave me was filled with love.

◆ ◆ ◆

"What do you mean, 'give her away'?" My mom asked, just as shocked as I anticipated, staring at me in disbelief while I stood with my back against the wall in our kitchen.

Daddy listened as I spoke, explaining everything to them just as I had to Ophelia.

There was silence for a long moment until Mom took a deep breath and asked, "Have you talked with Hailey at all about it?"

"No, Momma, I haven't. Daddy, I don't want to hurt or upset you. I just…I'm trying to do what you always told me to do: paying attention to my heart and using my mind to help me make the right decision. Both my heart and my mind are telling me this is the right thing to do."

"Nothing can replace Charlotte, honey, if that is what you are trying to do for her. It is not your job," my mom murmured, trying to understand.

"I am not trying to replace Charlotte; I am trying to help Hailey heal, just like Ophelia helped me and Daddy heal. I want to do that for her, and I have seen how much Ophelia loves her and how well they get along. I have so much here, with you and Daddy and all the horses at Hound Hollow that Miss Natalie lets me ride. Ophelia has done her work here. I think it is her time to go."

"How would you know that, Emma?" My mom asked, clearly confused at my certainty.

"Because," I replied, straightening my back and lifting my chin, "she told me."

"What do you mean she 'told you'?" My dad probed, perplexed.

"I talk to Ophelia. I know she can't answer in words, but I can feel what she is thinking. I don't know how to describe it. I just get a bad feeling when I am wrong about something and I feel at peace when I say something that is right. You always tell me to trust my instincts, Daddy. I don't know if it's instinct, or the Holy Spirit, but I *know* when I asked Ophelia to make a promise to me, I sensed that she agreed and I felt like she was at peace with it as well."

"What promise did you ask her to make?" my mom asked, curiously.

"I asked her to promise me that she would always look after Hailey, no matter what. I asked her to think of Hailey as an extension of me, and to always remember everything that we did together, and I told her that I loved her," I said, my lips quivering as tears streamed down my cheeks. "I told her that I would love her forever and that no one could ever take that away from her. She understood me Momma, I know it sounds crazy, but Ophelia *understands*."

My dad reached out to pull me into an embrace. His broad frame swallowed me up as my mom rubbed my back. I started to sob, my face resting against my daddy's chest as he soaked up my tears for me.

The next day after school, I called Hailey. Mom had already called her mom secretly during the day to let her know the offer was coming. Mom told me that Hailey's parents were shocked and humbled at our gesture, and I could go forward and offer Ophelia to Hailey.

There was nothing but silence when I asked Hailey if she would like to have Ophelia for her own. I explained that her parents had said it was all right and how I had thought long and hard about it, and even prayed about it. After a long silence, I checked in with her, "Hailey, are you there?"

"Yes, I'm here," she replied, her voice quivering with emotion.

"Well, what do you think?"

"I don't know what to say. Yes, oh my gosh, *yes!*"

We were both so happy in that moment. I knew I was doing the right thing, even though I was going to miss Ophelia terribly.

Hailey's tone became serious. "I do have one request and I hope it doesn't upset you or overstep at all."

"Sure, what is it? I asked, uncertainty tingeing my voice.

"Well see, ever since Charlotte passed and my time at Hound Hollow and with you, I have been thinking about getting a horse and I was hoping for a mare. I already had a name picked out for her. I wanted to call her 'Brielle'."

I paused. "Okay, sure, I guess that is okay, I mean I don't see why not." I searched for the right answer; the trouble was I wasn't sure what emotion I was feeling. "I just don't understand, why 'Brielle'?"

"Because," she replied, choking back her tears, "Brielle was Charlotte's middle name."

Chapter 8

Welcome to Babylon Stables
As told by Ophelia

The moment I walked into Babylon Stables I felt out of place. The assistant trainer at the farm, Stephanie, took my lead rope from the shipper that had spent the previous two days driving me nearly halfway across the country. As she did, he grinned at her and shared a few words about my manners, what I ate, and how much I drank in transit. As she walked me down the wide aisle, I tried to peer to each side, as many of the horses worked their way to the front of their stalls to see who the new horse was. I was intimidated by the ornate surroundings and by the presence of so many good athletes. Their grooming was exceptional; each was freshly body clipped and had manes that lay perfectly against the offside of their necks. I remember thinking how rough I must have looked to them. My coat was grungy from working up a sweat a few times on the trip, so despite how well Emma had seen me off, I hardly looked as though I belonged there.

I was ready to just get into my stall and get in a good roll. I was itchy from the dried sweat and I knew that would make me feel better. The size of the accommodations welcomed that, as the twelve-foot by twelve-foot stall was banked high in each corner with shavings. The fresh pine flew wildly around as I did a complete turnover, and after I scrambled back to my feet, I wiggled my whole body to shake off the sawdust.

Stephanie saw to it that my blankets were changed straight away to adjust to the Colorado winter. Just as the last strap was buckled under my belly, the head trainer, Tim, came in to have a look at me.

"So, you're the new girl, huh? Well, Hailey is sure going to be excited to see you."

"What time is she coming?" Stephanie asked as she left my stall.

"Oh, she'll be here right after school," Tim replied. "I think her dad is going to bring her over."

"What a lucky girl," Stephanie commented, "If I had a horse this nice at her age, I wouldn't know what to do with myself."

"She's pretty, isn't she?" Tim noted, scanning my outline. "She is plain, but she has a very classic look. How did her weight look when she had the blanket off?"

"She looked really good, actually."

"I talked to her last trainer, Natalie, and she said that the mare was pretty rough when she first got her, but evidently her last owner really took her time and did right by her."

"I still can't believe she just *gave* her to Hailey," Stephanie said, a puzzled look on her face.

"Yeah, right? I don't exactly know what the circumstances were, but Hailey sure could use a healthy distraction after the summer she had."

"No kidding," replied Stephanie. "I can't even imagine how that poor kid feels."

The way they talked about me made me feel a lot better, so I decided to try seeing myself in a more positive way. At Hound Hollow, I was labeled the mare that used to be no good but had improved greatly. Now, it seems, I fit in with good company and I liked the feeling that it gave me to be seen that way. Better yet, I liked it when I saw *myself* that way.

A scratching at the main door drew their attention. Stephanie jogged over to open it just enough to let a happy medium-sized dog push his way through to the warmth of the barn aisle.

"Brody, Brody!" Stephanie sang to the gleeful pup. He had tan fur on his ears and muzzle with matching tan legs and a line of tan across his brow that accented his short, black coat. He smiled broadly as he trotted through the barn like a prince, despite clearly being a mutt; a splotch of blue hair on his chest being the most obvious sign of his random breeding. He caught sight of me and broke past Stephanie and Tim in a frenetic scramble, making his way to my door where he braced his paws halfway up and lifted his nose to sniff feverishly at me. I recoiled a couple steps and snorted at him, to which he reacted by whipping back down the aisle, before Stephanie had a chance to correct him.

"What do you think of the new girl, Brody?" What do you think of Brielle?"

I lifted my head from the pile of hay I had just torn into. *Why did they call me Brielle?*

Not long after they left, Hailey came running into the barn, her dad, Thomas, walking behind her and grinning as Hailey hurriedly reached for my halter.

She came into my stall and gave me a big hug as the other horses looked on. All the worry and uncertainty that I felt on the trip out dissipated. Her essence was so similar to Emma's; she was pure and uninhibited with her emotions. I liked that, and her warmth was contagious.

72

"So, this is Brielle?" her dad asked her, gazing at me in wonderment.

"What do you think, Dad?"

"I have no idea what I am looking at, but she looks beautiful to me."

Tim came down the aisle and greeted Thomas and Hailey.

"Congratulations! How does it feel to be a horse owner?"

"Still getting used to the idea, I think."

"I'm sure you are going to do just fine. It looks like Brielle is settling in well. I have feeding instructions from Natalie, so we are in good shape on my end. Just let me know if you need anything else."

"Thank you so much Tim!" Hailey replied, her eyes never leaving me.

Hailey and Thomas were the last to leave the barn that first night. Hailey tucked me in; straightening my blankets, fluffing my hay, and giving me a molasses flavored treat that squished delightfully when I chewed it. The taste of it stayed with me, along with the sweet feeling of acceptance from my new owners and trainer.

I fell asleep soon after they left, but was awoken from my sleep by the distinct sound of a cat's nails grappling with fabric. My surroundings were illuminated by the moonlight shining through the window that was magnified by the glow from the newly fallen snow. Sitting atop the blankets that were hanging from the stall door was a tabby cat named Whinny whose pale green eyes complimented her soft, gray fur. She sat quietly watching me until an errant string from one of the blankets caught her attention, and she began batting at it. She sat on her hind end and stretched her paw towards the string, showing her puffy white chest that matched her four white paws. She would stop every few seconds to look at me as if to make sure I was watching; I got the sense she was trying to impress me and could also tell I welcomed the company. Each time she looked at me, she would soften her gaze and slowly blink. Her presence was warming, and I was pleased that she was with me. She would come to visit me nearly every night that I lived at Babylon, always making her way to me to stay for at least a short nap. She was accompanied at times by a fat, orange cat they called Ringo. He was not nearly as affectionate, but seemed affable, nevertheless. He would sometimes jump through the access hole for my grain, land evenly in my feed bucket, and in one motion, slide down the side of the large bucket and into the hay. He would always circle three times and plop himself sideways showing his large, white belly, which was always covered with hay and sawdust. Unlike Whinny, who enjoyed an occasional nuzzle from me, Ringo preferred nothing of the sort. He'd rather be observed and not touched, and if I came near him, he would flee into the night. I enjoyed his company as well, so I learned to leave him alone, and always made sure there was a pile of hay separate from my own where he could rest.

That first night at Babylon I had a lot of questions. I didn't quite know why they all thought so much of me, and I didn't know why my name was now 'Brielle'. But I did know I was loved, and that, to me, was an excellent start to my new life.

Chapter 9

Prayers for Bravado

The first several months at Babylon were lovely. While I missed Emma terribly, having Hailey as an owner was a wonderful experience. I was the envy of many of the other horses, whose owners were perhaps less sensitive to their true needs. Much like Emma, Hailey had tremendous work ethic and I never heard her complain, even on the coldest, darkest days of the Colorado winters. She seemed to sense that it was her company, kindness, and affection that I desired most. The rest of our time together, doing things like riding, lessons, and the competitions were very much secondary. I had felt like part of my heart was missing since I left Emma, and I knew Charlotte's absence was hurting Hailey so very, very much. I knew that if I could help her even the slightest bit, I was doing my part and that helping heal her would help soothe the heartache I had from missing Emma and my friends at Hound Hollow. I told myself that I would be my best with everything she asked of me so that she could concentrate on her own healing. I loved Hailey dearly, just as I did Emma. The chance to be able to care about two people this way made me grateful; it was this gratitude, in turn, that made me a happy horse.

I had the privilege of meeting so many wonderful horses at Babylon Stables. The horse that meant the most to me, however, was Bravado. I will always remember the first time I saw him; he arrived after a short stay at the quarantine center after being imported from Europe. He was to be Tim's signature horse that would gain him notoriety in the show jumping world. I listened as Tim and the owner of Babylon Stables, Bill, planned Bravado's future for him. I sensed Tim was genuine in his approach to the horses. He was thoughtful and caring with me in our sessions with Hailey and always spoke of the horses with compassion; even the ones that weren't in his training program and thus affecting his income. Bill, however, was different. I could tell he liked having us for the sake of being able to say he owned horses. And of course, he was always *so* concerned about the money. I remember my mother warning me about this; she thought all people only cared about the money, but I saw the world differently. I knew some people had their hearts in the right place. With Bill, however-I couldn't stand it when he was around! There were times when he would take his business partners down the aisle of the barn and brag about us. He would give us treats, trying to show them what a nice person he was. When no one was around, however, he was completely indifferent and always wanted to know what we were doing to make the farm money. He would ask Tim nitpicky questions, like how much we ate, and why we had so much bedding. He would even ask if we were winning; even if it wasn't his business, as was the case with Hailey and me. He was a human that repulsed me, so I would stand in the back of my stall and put my head down in the corner when he was around. He was just one of the reasons I worried for Bravado. He was so young and so naive when he came to Babylon. I tried to warn him about the various traps that he could fall into, but he believed deeply and for such a long time that his value was only in his performance rather than how he affected people's hearts. He was convinced that his existence on this earth was for the sport and for winning. I was there as his career flourished and I was truly excited for him and his future, but at the same time I knew one day his illusion would shatter. Winning was clearly going to his head, not his heart. Ironically, his heart was the main reason he was winning, not his mind or physical makeup. I thought he might start to recognize this when he started to break down and needed joint injections to keep performing at a high level, but he just wouldn't wake up to the empty dream he was chasing.

There was a series of events that occurred in Bravado's life that I watched unfold. The events were initiated with a decline in his performance from normal aging and wear on his body. Frustrated with failure at competitions, Bill threw a fit, which led to Tim calling Dr. Landing to come to the farm to give Bravado medication to help him get back to his best form. Bill's ego could not take being beaten and he pressured Tim constantly, which I sensed forced him to make decisions that were not in the best interest of the horses. Bill liked to control Tim by giving the impression that he could take everything away at any moment if things were not the way he thought they should be.

The injections worked, and Bravado felt terrific, but I had a terrible feeling the day he left for the Gateway show where he was to prove himself again. I was sure he was going back too soon after being laid up and that he was at risk for getting hurt. As it turned out, I was right.

Bravado sustained an injury that day that would only prolong his disillusion and cause intense suffering for everyone around him. It was such a terrible time in his life. I prayed and prayed for him, as did the other horse at the barn that cared for him. Ultimately, the injury would turn out to be a blessing for Bravado, as the circumstances sent him down a path that would eventually lead to him having a son, Whiskers. His son would one day symbolize how his true, enduring faith and persistence would ultimately triumph over every misgiving that his life had ever dealt him. But, that, of course is the story of a horse gone silent. This is my story, and I can assure you, I was anything but silent.

Chapter 10

Twice Removed

Greed has a way of punishing the person that indulges in it, and Bill was no exception. The trouble is it affects not only its transgressor, but everyone around them as well. Babylon Stables was built on financial sand, and when Bill's misdealings fell apart, so did the barn and everything that touched it. Tim, Stephanie, and all the grooms were all going to be out of work. Tim stayed on long enough to place all the training and sale horses in new homes, including Bravado, who had been sent to Thompson Therapeutic Riding Center. This meant that it was likely I was never going to see my friend again. I had grown so fond of him and I knew he cared deeply for me. I could hardly bear the thought of what was to come. I would miss him terribly, but I knew, at the very least, that I had Hailey and that she would certainly do her best to look after me.

I told Bravado the night before we were supposed to leave just how much I was going to miss him. It didn't feel like it was enough though, and I felt even worse when he saw how sad that I was. He was a brave horse and was always telling others to be strong and courageous, but he had such a soft heart. I was afraid what the separation would do to him emotionally. I was much more worried for him than I was for myself; I had Hailey. He had no one that he knew that he could rely on. If, heaven forbid, Hailey could no longer keep me, I always had the option to go back to Hound Hollow to live with Emma. Bravado didn't have that kind of security. It is tragically rare for a horse to know who they will be with forever. Many of us get passed down like clothes; every new owner having a different reason to use us, until finally we get to the point where a person may just stare at us, turn their head slightly sideways, and realize, that perhaps, we are no longer a fit for anyone that they know. If we are fortunate, we stay where we are, retired in a pasture with other horses until our last days. There is also a chance that we are sent down the road once more to a place less certain, with everything we have ever known and loved, just a lingering memory.

Just a few of us remained at Babylon, and the day finally came when I was to go to my new farm. After feeding that morning, Tim sat down on a hay bale, slumped against the wall with his head in his hands for close to an hour. The horses in the barn recognized his despair and we shared understanding glances over his head, knowing that there was nothing that we could do for him. He was so patient with us when we had training issues or didn't understand something. He tolerated Bill for our sake and stood up for us when we weren't performing our best. He had given his whole life to the horses at Babylon and he loved each and every one of us, only to have it stripped away from him due to someone else's greed. I kept my eyes on him, peering through the stall bars with a feeling of empathy for this young man whose dream had been destroyed.

The sound of Hailey's voice jolted me.

"Are you all set to go to your new home, Brielle?"

I came to the front of the stall to greet her. I tried not to act too excited because I could see Bravado and the other horses watching us. I nudged my nose towards her, and she reached under my chin for a bit of a scratch before heading to the tack room for my shipping wraps.

"Hi Tim. Are you doing okay?" she asked her trainer sympathetically as she passed him.

"Yes, I suppose. Thank you, Hailey."

She spent longer in the tack room than I expected and when she came out, Tim surprised her with a question.

"So, where did you decide to take your mare?"

"Oh, I thought my dad told you. We are taking her to Suzie Wells at Ironwell Farm."

Tim's shock put me on alert. "Suzie *Wells?* Hailey, what are you thinking?"

Hailey seemed honestly unaware why Tim was upset.

He could see this in her demeanor, and he reeled himself back in. "I'm sorry Hailey, what I meant was…" Tim paused. "What I meant to say was Suzie can be a little rough. You need to be careful."

"Okay. She seemed really nice when we took the barn tour. The farm is not nearly as nice as here, but she told us they were going to make improvements. She also told us she could help us reach our showing goals."

"I am sure she did," replied Tim sarcastically, Hailey didn't seem to notice his tone.

"Besides, you know we would go with you if you were to train somewhere else."

"Yea, thanks Hailey. I will let your dad know if my plans ever change. Just be careful with

Suzie-no matter where you go, just...be careful with your mare."

"Of course!" Hailey replied, trying to stay positive to cheer Tim up. I could tell she didn't know what to say.

The shipper showed up shortly after I was wrapped. Hailey took one last look around before she opened my stall door and clipped on my lead rope. I stepped out of my stall and closed my eyes briefly to signal a good-bye to Bravado. With guilt in my heart and hesitancy in my step, I made my way onto the trailer.

When we arrived at Suzie Well's farm, I felt uncomfortable immediately. They led me into my stall, which was dark and musty. There were cobwebs between the bars and there was no way to hang my head out. I felt trapped and uncertain. Hailey, her dad, and Suzie stood outside my stall to make plans for me.

"Do you have any more questions for us?" Thomas asked Suzie.

"Nope, you folks are all set. I will change her over to my feed program this week. I am sure she will settle in just fine."

Hailey broke away to get her tack organized. As she did, Thomas went on to Suzie.

"I want you to know that Brielle is *really* important to our whole family. I don't know if you are aware, but Hailey had a cousin—"

Suzie cut him off impatiently. "Yeah, they are all important to somebody. I will look after her, like I do everybody."

Thomas was taken aback by her dismissiveness, but he tried again. "Well, you see she had a cousin named Charlotte who passed away and this horse was given to her by a mutual friend to help Hailey heal. She is like a member of the family."

"Family member. Got it. Anything else? I need to go get ready for lessons tonight. I will let Hailey know when I can teach her next week. Just make sure you leave the board check before you go."

"Understood." Thomas replied stiffly. I could tell he was discouraged by her behavior, but his mood quickly changed when Hailey came back, excited to show him around.

"Come on Dad! I will show you the indoor ring."

"Okay, honey."

Like the good dad he was, he followed his optimistic daughter with a smile as she gave him a tour of my new home. I knew why she chose Suzie. Besides Suzie's ability to turn on her charm when she needed to, the farm was close to their home. The other farms were a much longer drive, and Hailey felt guilty having her parents drive her such a long way nearly every day. With both of them working, it made it difficult to get to the barn at a reasonable time after school. Ironwell Farm might not be the best, but it was the most logical choice. Hailey's parents didn't know enough about the horses to know any different, so they followed their daughter's lead. Unfortunately, Hailey was easily manipulated by Suzie and she really didn't know enough herself to realize that a little more time in the car would have been worth the trip.

◆ ◆ ◆

Over three years. Three *very* long years. That is how long I spent at Ironwell Farm with Suzie Wells. I watched in horror at the things she would do to horses when no one was around. I suffered while she screamed at us and beat us mercilessly. She would often take the new sale horses before they even had the chance to settle in and jump them until they limped, only to give them painkillers the next day to cover their lameness for unsuspecting customers. I listened as she berated her help and spoke maliciously behind the backs of her boarders and students. When in company of someone that could affect her pocketbook, she would readily turn on a fake version of herself that was just nice enough to keep the money coming.

Most days I couldn't understand how Hailey and the other riders couldn't see what I and the other horses saw. It was like they were unconscious to it or had just become inured to what was going on around them.

After my first few months at the farm, Hailey and her parents went back east to visit Charlotte's family. I worried, knowing that I wouldn't see them for several days. I decided just to keep to myself and behave the best that I could as to not upset Suzie. That is when she was her worst: when the owners were away. She would skimp on the hay and wouldn't bother to clean the water buckets or scrape the wet spots out of our stalls. Sometimes, she would walk right past us and not even feed us our grain, or if she did, it was just a handful. On the third day of Hailey's absence, Suzie had left the farm with the trailer to get a sale prospect. I scrounged the ground for what little hay was left and then fell asleep standing up in the corner of the damp stall; the reek of ammonia wafting from under me. I was awoken by the sound of the trailer coming down the driveway. Suzie lumbered her corn-fed physique out of the truck and made her way to the trailer door. She reached in and untied the horse and walked to the back of the trailer to drop the ramp. She let the ramp slam against the ground, unlatched the butt bar holding the horse in, and seconds later the passenger came swiftly backwards out of the side by side style trailer. Suzie snatched the lead rope and walked him briskly down the barn aisle. I pressed my nose against the raw stall bars and peered through, my eyes wild when I saw who was at the end of the shank.

"Bravado!" I whinnied, whipping around my stall in a frenzy.

"Brielle!" he exclaimed back.

Suzie shrieked a correction that sent me to the back of my stall, and I winced as she pulled unnecessarily hard on Bravado's lead shank, sending his head back and up towards the low, cobweb laden ceiling. I glared at her, full of hate. I hoped that Bravado couldn't see it. I didn't want to tell him what it was *really* like here. I was afraid to scare him. She stalled him close to me, so once she left the barn for the night, we were able to talk. I could tell by the way he looked at me that he was concerned for me, but he didn't say anything about it. It was the anger and fear that I had living inside me that was compromising my well-being. I knew by then that this is just how life worked at Ironwell. There was no fighting it.

I explained to him how I had ended up here and told him how she was not a real horseman, like Tim and Stephanie. I also advised him to stay in line so he wouldn't get hurt. I would soon regret that advice, because it did the opposite of what I had intended it to do. The next day Suzie took him to the outdoor ring with a couple of her working students. I was turned out in a nearby paddock where I could watch them work. They started jumping him almost immediately with nearly no warm-up. First a large cross-rail, then a vertical, then an oxer.

"Go up two holes!" Suzie grunted.

He came towards the oxer, following my advice to be obedient under all circumstances. He cleared it handily.

"Go up two!" she repeated portentously, a malicious grin holding her cigarette in the corner of her mouth as she watched her investment run down to the jump once more.

This went on for three days. On the third day, he looked as though he was running out of power. Feeling that he was depleted, the young rider pulled him up and looked at Suzie.

"I think he feels good Suzie. I feel like he has probably jumped enough."

"Not hardly. And why don't you let *me* make that decision. I'm the trainer, aren't I?"

The girl in the tack was clearly without means. I could see that she just wanted the chance to ride and be around the horses. Suzie gave her that, but she also took advantage of her good nature. As Suzie Wells did with everyone else, she was just good enough to the girl to keep her coming back and would then manipulate her to her advantage.

"Yes, sorry Suzie. Come back on the left lead?"

"Yea, more canter this time, he looks dull tonight. Lay a stick on him and send him up out of the corner."

"Okay, Suzie."

The girl did as she was told, and Bravado came down once more, and cracked his back hard in the air to make his best effort possible. The girl lost her balance with his hard jump. Suzie rolled her eyes at her and turned away.

"That's good enough," she remarked as she headed for her house, "you probably shouldn't ride this one anyway."

"I tried," she replied, discouraged.

"Just put him up for the night. I will just have to get on him tomorrow when no one is here."

"Should I wrap him?"

"Nah, just stick him in his stall with his cooler. I will deal with him later."

Later never came. The next day Bravado was sore and stiff when he came out of his stall. We all looked on sympathetically as Suzie had her riders send him to the ring anyway. He went down to one jump, landed on the other side and started to limp.

"Are you freaking kidding me?" Suzie sneered. "You piece of…"

She was on the phone with the horse dealer, Arthur, who sold him to her. They exchanged words as the rider took Bravado back to the stall.

"Should I cold-hose his legs?" she asked as Suzie came into the barn, fuming.

"No. Just leave him. He is going down the road in a hurry anyway."

The young girl bit her lip, clearly holding back tears.

"Don't worry," Suzie continued, "rats like him are a dime a dozen. We will get another one soon enough."

I held my breath as Bravado left the barn, the lights of Arthur's pickup truck casting menacing shadows over the parking lot and seeping into the aisle. The horses looked on as they loaded him in the trailer, a wicked bang and death-like rattle echoed through the barn as they closed the door.

"That trash can go to the killers for all I care," Suzie grumbled under her breath as she stalked past my stall.

God, I hope she didn't really just say that, I thought. Not the killers. I was overwhelmed with worry; my doom filled thoughts shattered by the shrill sound of Bravado's last scream to me. I screamed back, but I doubt he could hear me over the noise of the truck. He called out to me again. I circled my stall in a panic.

"Knock it off!" Suzie screamed. A couple other horses joined in, vainly trying to call encouragement to him as he vanished down the dark drive towards what was sure to be chaos. He was heading to the auction, and we all knew what that could mean. I got angry, so I started screaming even louder, this time pawing hard at the stall of my door.

Suzie made a dash at my stall. "I said, *knock it off!*"

I called out to him again. She picked up a pitchfork and hit my stall bars, the pernicious sound piercing the night and causing me to recoil. I wheeled and turned from her. I could see from the corner of my eye her anger burning through her eyes and into me.

"Turn around! You stupid mare!" she screamed.

I stood still, my back tense and ready to kick. I resisted the urge to let my hooves fly at her chest as she screamed again.

She slammed my door closed. "Fine. Have it your way. I will tell you right now, if you don't straighten out your act, I will make life miserable for you and your little princess of a rider. You just keep being that way. You pig!"

When she said "pig", I whipped around with my ears pinned back, shook my head up and glared at her through the stall bars. I wanted so badly to take revenge on her. As the vengeful thoughts tried to take over, the memory of my promise to Emma sobered me. I had to protect Hailey and I had to keep my promise to Emma, even as it felt as though the vultures were circling me, waiting for me to give up. In that instant I knew what I had to do to survive. I had to stay hopeful, I had to stay faithful, and I had to keep my heart filled with love. I had to be my best for Hailey's sake, and I had to pray every day for a way out.

Chapter 11

The Seven Vultures

My mother told me about the vultures when I was very young. On the rare occasion that she did advise me; it was nearly always in ways of dread and of the terror that life may bring.

"The vultures are everywhere, Ophelia," she had warned me. "I'm not talking about the ones that we see circling when one of us dies in a field, I mean the seven vultures of life," she lamented ominously.

"Everyone faces at least seven vultures in their life. You need to be ready. A vulture can come into your life in the form of a person who is filled with anger or hate and attack you outwardly. Other times, a vulture can take a hold of you from the inside, using one of the seven deadly sins, like pride, envy, greed, or wrath. It will tear at your heart and change you. It will strip you of your innocence and cloud your judgment. It will fill you with strife. No matter what, you can expect them to come and test you."

"What can I do, Momma? How can I keep them away?"

She looked away as she had the habit of doing and said quietly, "Nothing, Ophelia. Nothing. The vultures are always circling you; you just can't always see them."

Every day after Bravado left the farm, I thought about the vultures. For the next couple years, my own vultures took up residence inside me as I battled Suzie's noxious presence. I was resentful and filled with hate towards her. I was angry about my circumstances. I fought so hard against this evil but was depressed and unsure of myself most of the time. I stayed strong for Hailey, who somehow stayed unconscious to Suzie's ways. Everything was 'good enough', and somehow Hailey and her parents were accepting of the way things were. I realized that I had become the same way. It became the normal way of life for us. I think the horses accepted it as a way to survive. I think the people accepted it because they were being manipulated. There were people that would get wise to Suzie and leave, but somehow, she made it difficult for them to speak up. She was a masterful manipulator and short of kicking her teeth in, there was nothing a horse could do except take it.

Ironically, the more we lost at the horse shows, the happier I became. I could tell that Hailey's parents, especially her dad, were aggravated at our poor placings and it was clearly because of Suzie's decisions, not because of Hailey or me. Her parents were the best kind; they only wanted her to be safe and be happy, the results at the shows were secondary. Despite this humble approach, Thomas was clearly starting to question things. He had been travelling with work the first couple years we were at Ironwell, but he was home more now so he was able to come to the shows to watch. He didn't like what he saw. He approached Suzie at the barn after a lesson to question her.

"Suzie, can I ask you something?"

"What can I do for you?"

"I am wondering why Brielle and Hailey have been struggling at the shows."

"Why do you think they are struggling?" She retorted.

"That is why I pay you," he replied bluntly, taken aback at her tone.

"Maybe your kid and this mare are not the right match."

Thomas stared at her, clearly holding back a furious response.

"Sometimes kids grow out of their horses. I have others available, if you want to try one. You could just trade her in. Look at it as a 'trade-up.'"

"Do you remember *why* we have Brielle?" he asked her, monitoring his tone with all his will.

"Something about a cousin, right?" she answered dismissively.

"Right," he answered. And as he walked away, he commented expressionlessly, "You know Suzie, sometimes kids grow out of their trainers too."

"What was that?" she asked.

"Nothing Suzie, thanks for your time."

Thank God, I thought gratefully, *thank God he is starting to see through her.*

Suzie put up a good front for a few more months. She could sense that Thomas was not happy with her, so she started to treat Hailey special to gain her favor in case her dad started to hint about leaving. She would praise her more than the other riders in the lessons and started asking her to get on the sale horses. I knew what she was doing. She was trying to get Hailey to fall in love with another horse so she would forget about me. Hailey didn't see it, but I could. We all saw it.

Suzie was the worst vulture I had ever faced. She was the worst because she had a way of creating intangible vultures inside me that changed my character and my way of thinking.

At times, I felt completely disconnected from all of the important lessons that I had learned from Emma and Julia. I could feel that part of me leaving and I hated it. Somehow, I just couldn't help but be consumed with anger and I had no room left for what was good and right. I knew I was changing, and it was starting to make me weak and hollow; I was perfect prey.

Fall arrived and I remembered with ambivalence that this was the time of year that Emma had given me to Hailey years ago. A cold front had moved in over the mountains and I stared solemnly through the bars of the stall. I thought of Emma. I thought of the wonderful times we had and the care we received at Hound Hollow. Those memories filled me with warmth, despite the thin layer of shavings underneath me and the empty hay bag in front of my nose. I fell asleep as the chilly air drifted through the windows. I started to dream; I dreamt of a trail ride with Emma around Hound Hollow. I saw the corn on the horizon, I felt the creek water splashing my belly and I heard Emma's precious giggle as we made our way through the complex pine forest that she loved so dearly. My dream turned to me lying down comfortably in the stall at Hound Hollow, the sound of the crickets and toads singing their summer song as I rested peacefully. Then morning, it was such a sweet sight; Natalie walking down the barn aisle, looking approvingly in at us as she fed us our morning grain; speaking encouraging words to each of us as she passed by.

Then, the sound of Suzie's scratchy, sinister voice outside my stall pulled me violently out of my dream and back to reality. My vulture had arrived for the morning feeding, and she looked dreadfully hungry.

Chapter 12

Good Night Calebo

"What is this?" Suzie howled at a roan pony named Truman in the stall across from me. She investigated his stall and pulled the door back.

"You dummy! What is wrong with you?" she yelled at the frightened pony as he cringed away from her.

Truman had accidentally knocked over his water bucket in the night, causing it to soak his bedding. When he turned away from her, she took a lead rope and whipped it at him. "Turn around when I walk in the stall! You stupid brat of a pony!"

He pressed himself in terror up in the corner of the stall and she stomped out and slammed his door behind her. The rest of us nervously snorted and spun, hoping that was the worst of what was to come that day. Then, after feeding she came to my stall to take me outside for turn-out. I stood quietly as she slipped my halter on and went to carefully follow her out. She tripped clumsily on the threshold of my stall, which caused me to fly back away from her. I avoided injury when I narrowly missed hitting my head on the frame of the stall, but the lead rope slid through her hand so fast that it scorched her skin. She got up as fast as her bell-like body would allow and turned at me in a fit of rage; hay and manure from her unkept barn aisle covering her front side.

"Watch it you pig! Watch it! You know what, why don't we put the shank on you today?"

She slipped the metal chain over my nose. I knew to stand still and do nothing because I didn't want her to use it; a shank could be incredibly painful in the wrong hands. She looked at me with her eyes filled with fire, as she took the shank and ripped downward on my nose. I flew back and reared up, slamming my head on the rafter. She shanked again. "Stupid pig! You got it now! Stupid pig!" she yelled over and over as if a demon had possessed her; the vile anger from her soul transmitting itself onto me through a painful array of blistering shanks that caused searing pain through my skull.

When she finally started to let up, I backed all the way to the corner of my stall, trembling in fear and pain. I was petrified; uncertain of what she was going to do to me next. I heard a car pull into the driveway, and I believe to this day it's the only thing that saved me. Susie looked outside to see who it was and I sensed her immediate panic.

It was Hailey and Thomas. *Thank God!* I thought to myself. *Thank God.* She tried to quickly pull my halter off and get out of my stall before they entered the barn, but I was so head shy that I flew back again, making it impossible for her to get to it. She gave up, shot me a disdainful look, and abruptly left my stall.

"Good morning Thomas! Good morning Hailey! What are you two doing here so early?" she asked so sweetly that even Hailey, in her naïve way, sensed something was off.

"Just here to give Brielle a quick grooming before me and my folks head out of town overnight. Remember? I rescheduled my lesson for later in the week."

"Oh, right. Of course, I remember. Well, I was about to turn her out, but I will let you do that."

"Okay."

Thomas eyed me suspiciously; he could tell something was wrong.

"Why is she standing in the back of the stall like that?" He asked.

"She always does that in the morning, you are just never here then," Suzie answered looking away from them and down the aisle. "Why don't you clean your tack first, Hailey?"

"We don't really have time, just here for a quick grooming. Wait, why is she sweating? Hey girl, are you okay?"

Hailey came into my stall and walked towards me. I cringed away. Even though it was Hailey, I still felt an instinctive need to be cautious. Thomas made his way into the stall with Hailey and reached towards my nose. He went to pet me and put his hand right where the metal shank had scraped me. The moment he touched me, I flew back to avoid the pain. My body shook with the fear that had overtaken me.

"Whoa girl," Hailey murmured comfortingly. "Daddy, something is not right."

"It sure isn't, Hailey. Go ahead and take care of Brielle."

Thomas turned to Suzie. "What happened this morning?"

"What do you mean? Nothing. She is just being a chestnut mare. They are all the same. Unpredictable and nasty at will."

"That doesn't fly with me. She has never acted like this before."

Hailey broke in. "Daddy, Brielle is bleeding. The top of her head is cut and so is her nose."

"How did she get hurt?" Thomas pressed Suzie further.

"I don't know. Maybe she somehow scraped her head on her feed bucket. It's not that bad, here, let me take a look."

Suzie walked into my stall with the chain shank still in her hand. As she came closer the metal caught the light and spooked me, as I was already on high alert. I flew back and hit my head again. Then I spun away from her in dread, nearly knocking her and Hailey over.

"See, just a chestnut mare! What a pig!"

Then I saw something that I never expected or could have foreseen. Hailey woke up.

"*What* did you just call her? Did you call her a pig?"

"She is, she is just a pig of a horse!" Suzie replied flatly, without her normal flattery.

Hailey advanced in deliberate steps, backing Suzie out of the stall. Suzie cowered against the other side of the aisle as the young woman that had once been so submissive, looked as though she was about to put her hands around Suzie's throat.

"Her name is Brielle. You got that? Her name is Brielle! And you will never, *ever,* go near her again!"

Thomas stood by silently, clearly proud of his little girl for standing her ground in the face of evil.

Shaken, she turned to her father. "Dad, we need to call the vet."

"You got it, Hailey."

"We also need to call the farm, Hopewell Ridge, we were talking about. *Today*."

"Most certainly," Thomas replied, peering at me with concern.

"Suzie, I expect you to leave us alone. We will be gone by the end of the day."

Suzie didn't reply. She just circled the barn the rest of the morning, grumbling disdainfully to herself. Hailey waited with me until the veterinarian came and looked after my wounds, which were thankfully superficial. Shortly thereafter, a shipper arrived, and I was on my way to my new home.

The ride to Hopewell Ridge was a quiet one. A large hay bag was set in front of me in the clean, bright trailer. I was grateful to be by myself; I needed time to process everything that I had gone through that day. It was so frightening to think of those moments with Suzie. My thoughts wandered as if at their own will and started to replay all the evil that I had endured in my life. I couldn't make the desperate and anxious feelings stop.

I thought of my time with my mother and what she tried to teach me about how cynical everyone is in the world. How she made it clear to me that there was no point in looking forward. As I thought of those words my heart ached with a deep, solemn sadness that spread through my body and left me feeling weak. Next, my mind went to my time at Lydia's and I could see the word 'pig' coming from Karen's mouth as she spewed her venomous hatred towards me. And then, finally to Hound Hollow. Somehow, despite all that Natalie, Emma and her family did for me I just couldn't see the good in anything. I wanted to justify what Suzie had done to me somehow. I wanted to find the good in it, but it was like my mind had control of me, instead of me having control of my mind. My mother's voice kept pushing against the good, her warnings of the vultures darkening my thoughts even more. All I could see was the evil; the money, the greed, the use of the horse for nothing but man's gain, and I started to wonder. I started to lose hope.

The truck pulled into the drive at Hopewell Ridge. I had no idea what to expect. I only knew what Hailey had mentioned quietly to her father, and I had recalled from the shows that all of Mary's horses looked well, but that was all.

Hailey backed me quietly off the trailer and I immediately snaked my neck around to take in my new surroundings.

Mary stood waiting for me, seeming delighted that I had arrived.

Hailey introduced us. "This is my mare; her name is Brielle. Where would you like her to go?"

"Oh Hailey, she is lovely! There is a stall open for her next to the black horse on the end. Just watch the barn cats. They can be a little wild!"

Mary was trying to make Hailey comfortable, which made me feel a bit more at ease, until I heard an eager whinny from the far end of the barn. My heart began to race. Again, the whinny. I knew that voice. Wait, I thought, could it really be? Could it really be *him*?

I arched my neck and lifted my tail as I began to jig sideways towards the barn, consumed with what I thought I had just heard. Hailey looked up at me, puzzled as she tried to manage me.

"I'm so sorry Mary," Hailey said apologetically, "she's never like this."

"Bravado!" I called in hopeful delight. "Bravado!"

I settled myself for Hailey's benefit as we crossed the threshold into the barn, allowing just a quiet prance to my step as she walked me down the aisle. My arrival caused quite a commotion, as the other horses spun in their stalls and leaned over their stall guards to have a look at me. Two barn cats scurried quickly past me as a dozen or so barn swallows dove riotously through the air.

We got to the end stall and then there he stood. As Bravado's eyes met mine, I pulled the lead from Hailey to put my nose to his. Hailey gently tugged on my lead and turned me into my stall. Mary put only the stall guard up, which was just above my chest and allowed me to lean into the aisleway to have a look at my new surroundings. I ignored everything; the commotion dissipated, and my thoughts cleared as I locked my eyes with my very best friend.

I listened as Mary explained to Hailey who Calebo was, and how he had once been known as Bravado. I enjoyed hearing the story from Mary's perspective, especially as Mary told the tale of his remarkable life in such detail. They chatted on in cheerful astonishment at the connection between Bravado and me after all these years.

I was awestruck at where my fate had delivered me. I realized in that moment that things really *could* be different after all.

Hailey came to me in my stall on a frigid November afternoon as the sun set, taking the last bit of warmth with it as it disappeared behind the hedgerow of sycamore trees that bordered Hopewell Ridge. She adjusted my blankets carefully, and then tenderly wrapped her slim, young arms trustingly around my neck. She breathed in the smell of my hair and squeezed me tight as she rubbed a tear-streaked cheek against my soft coat.

"Thank you, Brielle," she whispered. "Thank you for all that you have done for me. I am so sorry that I didn't realize how awful Suzie was to you. I wish I had seen it sooner. I promise I will never let anything happen to you again. You will stay here *forever*, I promise."

I wrapped my neck over her shoulder, hugging her back the only way I could. I realized just how much I loved her and that I would do anything I could for her as well. After Hailey left my side and went home, Bravado and I talked softly together.

"It has been quite a journey, hasn't it?" He asked.

"Yes, it really has," I replied.

"What has mattered most to you with everything you have gone through?"

"Up until I moved to Hopewell Ridge, I wouldn't have been able to answer you. At least not in a positive way. But now I can. It's helping people; helping the ones with the *good* hearts that lose their way. Being a part of their lives and enabling them to find their way back to what is beautiful and right in this world. That is what matters most to me."

"I agree." he answered, his voice content and peaceful.

"By the way, what do you want me to call you? Bravado or Calebo?"

"You can call me Calebo. That is who I am now. And what about you? Are you good with being Brielle?"

"Yes, I most certainly am," I replied warmly, "my name defines who I am. It defines where I get my strength."

"Well, then, good night, Brielle."

"Good night, Calebo."

We both slept soundly the whole night through. Our bellies were full of hay and ample straw bedding kept us warm, while the promise of a sweet breakfast was near. Then, the most wonderful thing occurred. As night turned to dawn, the rising sun cast a light through our windows and down the barn aisle, bringing the promise of an unusually warm November day. With it came two red breasted robins, flitting and diving through the air; chatting cheerfully about everything that is pure, right, lovely, noble, and admirable. And everything, as it were, fell perfectly into place.

"Finally, brother and sisters, whatever is true, whatever is noble, whatever is right, whatever is pure, whatever is lovely, whatever is admirable-if anything is excellent or praiseworthy-think about such things." ~ Philippians 4:8

Thank you for reading *Brielle's Promise*, the third book in the *Horse Gone Silent* trilogy. I hope that the story touched your heart.

If you loved the story and have the time, please leave a review on Amazon. It makes *such* a big difference when you do. Thank you.

Horse Gone Silent Trilogy

Horse Gone Silent◆Sycamore Whispers◆Brielle's Promise

Additional Titles by the Author

Color Me Real Coloring Books

The Pony That Wouldn't Whinny

Acknowledgements

I would like to thank the following people for their love and support of this meaningful work.

My darling wife Carice

My son Kevin

My daughter Kaydy

Gale Rosencrance

Phyllis Jean Shoemaker

"Canadian" Bob McDonald

Louise Kass

My editor Catherine Stone

My neighbor, Dave Smith. You proved that timely advice and kind words can do far more than most people can ever imagine.

Made in the USA
Middletown, DE
07 October 2024